TRUNDLEBERRY MANOR

MR. BOUNCER'S HOUSE

FIRE STATION

BLODGER'S GATEHOUSE

SIGMUND SWAMP'S HOUSE & BOATHOUSE

FERNYBANK FERRY

BROCK GRUFFY'S SHOP

BRAMBLE'S FARM

CHURCH

VICARAGE

RAILWAY STATION

P.C. HOPPIT'S HOUSE

POLICE STATION

DR. BUSHY'S HOUSE

N
W   E
S

This book belongs to:

....

MR. RUSTY'S NEW HOUSE

Written & Illustrated by John Patience

DERRYDALE BOOKS
New York
Copyright © 1984 by Fern Hollow Productions Ltd
This 1984 edition is published by Derrydale Books,
distributed by Crown Publishers, Inc.
Printed in Italy
ISBN 0-517-427877

One morning Rufus Rusty woke up
with something dripping on his forehead.
PLIP PLIP PLIP.
"Oh no!" cried Rufus to his brother
Redvers who was in the lower bunk.
"The roof is leaking."
"Never mind," giggled Redvers.
"I'm quite dry down here!"

Rufus leapt out of his soggy bed and ran to tell his
mother and father, but they were already running
around with pots and pans trying to catch the rain, which
was leaking into their bedroom. It was the same in
Dusty's room.

"It's hardly worth having a roof at all if it's going to leak
like this!" said Mrs. Rusty.

Eventually Mr. Rusty managed to find enough pots and pans to catch all the drips. Then, after eating his breakfast, he set off for work at the railroad station, where he was the engine driver. As he left, Mr. Rusty closed the front door behind him—and it fell off!

All day long things went wrong with Mr. Rusty's house; soot fell down the chimney, the windows stuck and wouldn't open and Mrs. Rusty fell through the floorboards which had become rotten.
"Oh, I wish we had a new house," she moaned.

That night there was a terrible thunder storm.
Lightening flashed around the sky and it rained cats and
dogs.

In the morning the River Ferny, which had become
swollen with all the rain, overflowed and rushed down
into the hollow where Mr. Rusty's house stood. The
water crept up higher and higher until, at last, Mr. Rusty
and his family had to climb up onto the roof.

When Mr. Periwinkle the Postman came riding down the lane and saw Mr. Rusty and his family all perched on their cottage roof, he was so surprised that he fell off his bicycle.

"Don't worry, Mr. Rusty," cried Mr. Periwinkle, scrambling to his feet. "I'll ride over to the fire station and get Alphonso Duff and Mr. Bouncer—they'll know what to do."

The Fern Hollow firemen soon arrived
and began the rescue operation,
extending the ladder on top of the fire
engine all the way across the floodwater
to the Rusty family's roof.

Rufus and Redvers thought
it was all great fun, until
they both lost their balance
as they were climbing along
the ladder and fell
in the water!

Mr. Prickles had been watching the rescue and, realizing that the Rusty family would now have nowhere to live, he invited them to stay with him for a while. The kind hedgehog soon made a nice warm fire and Mrs. Prickles gave each of the Foxes a bowl of steaming hot soup.

Later in the day Mr. Rusty heard a lot of
noise outside Mr. Prickles's house and
went outside to see what was happening.
A little further down the lane Brock
Gruffy and a few other animals had
started to build Mr. Rusty a new house.

Mr. Rusty set to work himself at once.
There was plenty to be done; hammering
and sawing, cement to make and bricks to
lay. It was a lucky thing for Mr. Rusty and
his family that they had so many good
friends to help them.

It took quite a long time to build the house, but each day a little more was done. The walls grew up and the roof was put on.

The tiles were laid and the windows and doors were fitted, and at last Mr. Rusty's new house was finished.

Of course, all the furniture from the flooded house was useless, but Mrs. Rusty's friends each gave her bits and pieces from their own homes, and Mr. Chips the woodman arrived with lots of tables, chairs and cupboards which he had made.

That night Mr. Rusty held a house-warming party to thank all his friends for their kind help. It was a very jolly party. The air around Mr. Rusty's new house was filled with the sound of singing and laughter and the lights of the windows twinkled merrily in the darkness.

Fern Hollow

MR CHIPS'S HOUSE

MR WILLOWBANK'S
COBBLERS SHOP

MR CROAKER'S WATERMILL

STRIPEY'S HOUSE

SCHOOL

THE JOLLY VOLE
HOTEL

RIVER FERNY

MR ACORN'S
BAKERY

MR RUSTY'S HOUSE

MR PRICKLES'S HOUSE

POST OFFICE

BORIS BLINKS'S
BOOKSHOP

MR TWINKLE'S
HOUSE

MR TUTTLEBEE'S
SHOP

MR THIMBLE'S
TAILORS SHOP

WINDYWOOD